ANIMAL POWER

THE AMAZON

IRENE LARN

PUBLISHED BY

MINNETONKA, MN 55305

WWW.SIGMASBOOKSHELF.COM

ANIMAL POWER BY IRENE LARN

Cover design contains public domain imagery from PublicDomainPictures.net.

Amazon basin map image from Wikipedia featuring artwork from KMusser. Image licensed under the Creative Commons Attribution-ShareAlike 3.0 Unported.

Additional chapter heading images courtesy of Pixabay.com.

Printed in the United States of America

First Printing 2019

ISBN 978-0-9996577-4-4

Dedicated to
Fiona

Caracas
VENEZUELA
Orinoco
Georgetown
Atlantic
Ocean
Bogotá
GUYANA
COLOMBIA
Vaupés
Branco
Boa
Vista
Macapá
Apaporis
Negro
Trombetas
Peru
Jari
Caquetá
Japurá
Amazon
Pará
Quito
Belém
Putumayo
Santarém
ECUADOR
Napo
Manaus
Pastaza
Trigre
Iquitos
Madeira
Tapajós
Iriri
Marañón
Javary
Juruá
Purus
Juruena
Teles Pires
Huallaga
Ucayali
Xingu
Pucallpa
Machado
Arinos
Tocantins
Rio Branco
Porto
Velho
Acre
Madre de Dios
Araguaia
Tambo
Ene
Guaporé
Mantaro
Apurimac
Lima
Cusco
Beni
Mamoré
Brasília
PERU
La Paz
Grande
Cochabamba
Santa Cruz
BRAZIL
Pacific
Ocean
BOLIVIA
Rio de
Janeiro
São Paulo

Chapter 1

The Amazon

Amber dropped a five dollar bill into her backpack, then zipped it shut and swung it onto her back. The dark-haired, freckle-faced girl lived on a shabby, little street that looked exactly like the one before it, and the one after that. On these boring streets were boring houses, each model looking exactly like the others. Amber lived on Cloud Street. Hers was the third house on the left.

Amber's backpack sagged as she left the house. *Why did I pack so many stuffed animals?*

Today was the sixth grade's week-long camping trip. They were going to South America to visit the Amazon. Amber had been looking forward to this trip since she was four years old when her mom had taken her to the Minnesota Zoo's rainforest. She had loved it so much at the time she expressed the desire to have a birthday party there, and that year she did. Amber had wanted to go on a trip to the Amazon ever since.

By the time she was in fourth grade, she had filled a whole notebook with the facts she knew about the Amazon. The 350 page notebook contained 4,345 facts about the Amazon, and a play she had written when she was in the fifth grade. She was very proud of this play. It was about the Amazon

1

because why else would she put it in the notebook? She had memorized it from beginning to end.

Along with the notebook, she intended to bring everything on the Amazon trip list she made when she was four. She had already packed a folded-up duffel bag that would hold all the interesting things she would collect in the Amazon, an empty notebook in which she would write down her observances, a mini telescope, a flashlight, a camera, a map, a guide book called *How to Live in the Rainforest,* and tons of stuffed animals. They included: a baby tiger, a kitten, an elephant, a bunny, a horse, a puppy, a monkey, a turtle, a bluebird, a squirrel, a hedgehog, a rare salamander, a penguin, an owl, and a lion! She also planned to bring a sleeping bag, pillow, and suitcase for all her clothes.

Amber couldn't wait to get to school that day. The first thing she was planning to do was run up to her best friend, Raya, and make sure she knew how excited she was. Raya had been Amber's best friend since kindergarten, and this year was in her sixth grade class at Newberry Middle School. The girls' favorite thing to do together was to go camping. They always took Raya's grandpa's camper, and brought along whomever's parents could come.

Amber walked down a narrow street to the main road where the bus stop was. Had she missed her bus? She hoped not. Amber looked curiously around as traffic zoomed by, ruffling her long, curly black hair. Amber was bold and full of adventure, and couldn't wait for her trip.

Then Amber remembered that her class play was being performed before they took their huge trip. She was excited about it, but nervous as well. She had thirty-one lines in it, and she was glad that they were all memorized.

Amber was not afraid to be on stage at all! Just a little nervous. The play she was in was titled *Fire.* She played

Fire, a horse that could talk, and the play's main character. She had really wanted the role and was so excited when she found out she had gotten it! They were performing first thing at eight thirty that morning. She wondered if Raya was nervous as well.

Finally, the school bus turned the corner, then drove up. It stopped in front of her, its brakes squeaking. The doors of the bus opened, and when the driver saw all the stuff she had brought with her he said, "Do you need help with all that?"

"Yes, please," she said, then handed the driver her suitcase, followed by the pillow and sleeping bag. She already had the backpack on and kept it with her as she climbed the stairs, then made her way to the back of the bus. She left her other stuff up front.

When she took her seat, she intended to practice her lines for the school play, but the other passengers were loudly chattering away, making it hard for her to concentrate on the lines running through her head, though Amber wasn't in the least bit annoyed. Nothing could ruin the best day of her life!

After several minutes spent picking up the rest of the kids on the route, the bus screeched to a halt in front of her school. Amber got off and nearly ran to her classroom in excitement, tripping over her sleeping bag. "Oops," she said, then rearranged what she was carrying and raced towards the classroom.

"Sit down at your desk, Amber, you're late," said Ms. Clay. As the whole class looked on, Amber smiled and took her seat. She was kind of embarrassed.

"Okay, now that we're all here, we can get ready for the play. I need everyone to get into their costumes," announced Ms. Clay, motioning towards the back of the room as she waved the play script in her hand. Amber followed Raya to the back of the classroom where a metal rack on wheels stood. The costumes hung on hangers on the rack. Amber waited her turn in line, then when it was her turn, pushed a bunch of costumes aside before finally finding her brown and white Pinto costume. She took it off its hanger and put it on over her white tank top.

Once all the kids were in costume, Ms. Clay led the way down the hallway to the school auditorium. Once inside, the students made their way backstage. Amber sat down on a bench and twisted her thumbs. She was a little nervous as she listened to Ms. Clay announce their play to the audience.

"Today, on this fine, fine day, the sixth grade presents *Fire!*"

The audience clapped loudly as Ms. Clay left the stage. When Amber could no longer feel the stage vibrating from Ms. Clay's feet thumping down the steps, and the clapping had stopped, she knew it was her time to shine. She got up from her backstage bench, opened the curtain, and stepped onto the stage. Amber gasped. The audience was huge! She took a deep breath, and was ready with her first line when Raya entered the stage in her butterfly costume.

"Hi, I can't believe I haven't seen my owner in days," Amber said, then she thought of her next line.

"Which owner?" Raya asked.

"I only have nine hundred," Amber answered, trying her best not to laugh.

"Nine hundred? But last time I saw you, Fire, you had only three hundred owners," Raya said, as she pretended to be confused. "How do your owners multiply so fast?"

"Because every person who buys me only wants me for tests and science because I can talk. What's the big deal? They can talk, so why are they so surprised that I can?" Amber asked, then waited for Jack to enter.

After a pause of silence, they heard a creak as Jack stood up, left the bench, then came on stage. He walked forward until he stood between Amber and Raya, then he said, "After a long, hard trek through the woods, they came to a babbling brook where a young girl walked picking blueberries." After he said that, Jack walked backstage.

May took his place on stage. She was wearing a white dress, sprigged with pink flowers and green leaves. Her hair was done into two nice braids that were tied with pink ribbons. She sat down every so often, setting down the basket she was carrying, and pretending to pick blueberries from the blueberry bush scenery that was scattered around the blue, cloth river.

May stood up all of a sudden, pretending to be startled by seeing a horse. She then cautiously started walking towards Amber. "Hi, do you need something?" Amber asked.

May pretended not to hear her. She kept creeping cautiously towards Amber and looked around nervously.

"Why can't she hear us?" Ray asked.

"I don't know, but I think it has something to do with the fact that she is not an animal," Amber said in a matter-of-fact tone.

"Maybe, Raya presumed.

"Hi there pretty horse. What's your name?" May asked.

"I'm the legendary horse, Fire!" Amber announced, then she pretended to remember. "Oh, yeah, she can't hear me."

"I wish I could have a horse like you, except—my father wouldn't allow it," May told the audience, then she pretended to jump as Bob came on stage, wearing baggy, tan jeans and a dark, old-time blue shirt.

"What are you doing near a horse!? I have told you a million times that you are not allowed around horses. It is unladylike," Bob scolded.

"But—but father!" May argued.

"Sorry, that's how it has to be! Do you want to be trampled by a horse like your mother?" Bob asked.

"No but—" May stammered.

"Then deal with it!" Bob shook his fist.

"But it wasn't the horse's fault. It was going too fast to stop in time," May said, but Bob had already exited.

"At least I can stay here long enough to name this horse," said May. "Hmm—I think I will name him Fire after his blazing coat." After May made that declaration, she left the stage at the same place where Bob had exited.

Amber came forward and enthusiastically said, "She figured out my name! I am Fire the legendary horse!"

After saying her line, Amber left the stage, and was soon followed by Raya. She then watched as Ms. Clay turned off the spotlights until everything was dark, except for a little sliver of light shining through the window. There was just enough light for Amber to see the stage through the curtain. She could see Bob and May carrying a chair onto the stage. Then they set it down, and went backstage again. When the light came back on, May was sitting in the chair. There was a basket with yarn in it at her feet, and she had started knitting. Bob entered, carrying a book under his arm.

"Hi, Anna. I got this book in the mail. One of our close relatives sent it, and I promised not to read it. Here," Bob announced, and handed the book to May. Amber watched through the curtains as May set down the knitting and received the book in her outstretched hands. She looked at the front cover, then looked wildly around.

"I'll just leave you to read then," Bob said, then returned backstage.

May looked down at the book and read the title. "*Fire, The Legendary Ghost Horse*. Hey wait! Wasn't Fire the horse I saw? Do you think I saw the legendary ghost horse? I think I did," May said in a matter-of-fact way because this was serious business.

Bella entered the stage. She was wearing a tight, white

dress with see-through sleeves. "Hello Anna, my daughter. If you want to find what you seek, follow your heart," Bella told her gently, then slowly left the stage.

There was a knock on the door painted on the scenery. It had hinges so it could actually open. Bob opened the door and said, "Time for school!"

"Uh—okay," May said anxiously, then left the stage. Bob followed her and the lights were dimmed until it was completely dark. Amber whispered, "Good luck," to May as she gathered her things (a desk, paper, and pencil), then returned to the stage. Amber knew that May usually had trouble with her lines in this scene, and took a deep breath. Georgia, Jack, Julian, Sophie, August, Joy, Tom, and Danny came on stage with her. They were also carrying desks, paper, and pencils.

Amber watched through the gap of the curtains as they all set up their desks as if they were in a classroom, then they all exited to grab chairs for their desks. Once the scene was set, they all sat down at their desks onstage, then the dimmed lights slowly brightened again until they were at full blast. Amber crossed her fingers in her lap and the scene began. All the students onstage pretended to be talking to one another. As Tracy entered the stage, Amber looked at Ms. Clay and saw that she was sitting tensely in her seat. *She must also know this isn't May's best scene,* Amber thought.

All the people who were playing students: Jack, Julian, August, Tom, Georgia, Sophie, Joy, and Danny, were wearing old-time clothes. Their costumes were nothing like Tracy's with her crazy, strict teacher glasses, and her long, black uniform. What she was wearing made her look important. Her shoes were black and shiny as if they had been polished at least one hundred times. She was carrying a pile of books in her arms, and had a pointing stick in her right hand.

Tracy passed out a book to each student then announced, "We will read this book together. We will each take turns reading a sentence."

Jack, who was to read the book first, said, "Deep in a forest near a marshy undergrowth of trees lay a little house made of stone." Jack then looked over at Julian, who read next.

"No one lived in this house for one particular reason: whenever anyone opened the door and got a glimpse inside, an angry dragon would breathe fire through the doorway, warning trespassers to beware."

Next, August took his turn in the reading. "As far as anyone knew, no one lived in this house, and the strange thing was that when someone said they had seen inside the house, and someone asked them about it, they seemed to forget what they had seen right when they tried to tell someone about it."

Tom took a breath, and was about to read when May said, "I didn't get a book!"

"Oh, sorry," Tracy said, not seeming to be sorry at all. Rather than handing May a book, Tracy then said, "Look at the time! It's time to switch classes kids."

May stood up angrily. "I didn't get a book, *and* you won't let me read! What's next, homework?"

"You are correct! Your homework is to read this book," Tracy said in a fake cheerful voice.

"Is that *our* homework too?" Sophie asked.

"No," Tracy said hotly.

Georgia gave May her book, and they all exited, taking their props with them. Amber knew that May had said her line wrong, but she was glad to see that it still made sense with the story line.

When the stage was cleared and the spotlight went dim, May re-entered with a chair. She set the chair down and sat on it. The spotlights brightened. In her lap, she had two books. One was *Fire the Legendary Ghost Horse.* The other was her homework book from school. May then spoke. "I need to read my homework book, but I really want to read *Fire the Legendary Ghost Horse.*"

Amber stood up from the bench, and entered the stage. She felt bold at first, but then scared after she saw the crowd once more. May gave a gasp of surprise at the sight of her.

"Would you like a ride?" Amber asked. May jumped up and down with excitement, then Bob entered.

"What are you doing?" he boomed. "Do not ride that horse!"

"Sorry father, but I'm going to ride him," May said determinedly.

Amber bent down so May could get on her back, then she gave May a piggy-back ride around the stage. Bob just stared at them. Then Amber stopped and let May climb off her back.

"You're—you're—alive!" Bob stammered.

"Of course I am!" May objected. "Father, can we keep him?"

There was complete silence for what felt like an eternity, then finally Bob said softly, "No! I'm sorry."

"But don't you see? Horses aren't dangerous. Mom being run over by a horse was an accident," May told him.

Bob looked down, and seemed to be thinking hard, then softly said, "Actually, I think you're right."

"Really?" May asked, surprised.

"Really. We can keep him," Bob said decidedly.

"Fire! Did you hear that? We can keep you. We can keep you!" May said excitedly.

Everybody in Amber's class now filed in from backstage, and they all formed a line and bowed. The crowd cheered. Amber saw her mother in the front happily clapping and cheering, and smiled. Then they exited, and all crowded the halls as they headed back to their classroom. Amber held Raya's hand excitedly.

When they got back to the classroom, the kids took off their costumes as quickly as they could and hung them back up on the hangers, then took their seats.

Chapter 2

The Plane

Once everyone in the class was in their seats, Ms. Clay made the announcement everyone was waiting for. "Okay kids. Now that all the costumes are put away, it's time for our field trip," she said. "Finn, Jack, Tom, and Danny, go gather your things and follow Jack's mom to her car. Joy, Raya, Amber, May, June, Bella, and Tracy, you are going in May's minivan."

Yes!" Amber thought. *I'm in the same car as Raya.*

"Bob, Julian, and August are going in my car, and Sophie and Georgia are going in Sophie's car."

"Can we go and find the people we are riding with now?" asked Julian, a short, blond-haired boy.

"Of course, but next time raise your hand," Ms. Clay said, glaring at Julian, who quickly looked away.

There was total chaos as the whole class rushed out of the classroom. Amber was so excited! She was the first to get her things together, even though she had the most to gather. She even reached the car first. Raya, who was hard on her heels, arrived second, followed by May, June, and Bella. Joy, who was a shy, red-haired girl who had joined their class just last year, arrived last. Her best friend, May, grabbed her hand when she arrived, and she smiled.

"Do I have everyone?" asked their driver, John, May's father.

"Yup," Amber answered. She was anxious to get going. A chilly wind blew Amber's long, black hair into her face when John opened the back of the minivan.

"You can put your luggage in here," he said. Once the kids had piled their suitcases in, John closed the hatch and said, "Okay, everybody in."

Amber was the first to get in. She climbed into the very back seat, then slid over to make room for Raya and Joy. May, June, and Bella sat in the middle seat. Once all the kids were in the minivan, John said, "Okay, everyone buckle up," then he slid the door closed and climbed into the driver's seat. He turned the key, then pulled into the line of cars waiting to head to the airport.

As they drove away, Amber looked out the back window, watching the school get further and further away. When they stopped at a light, she recognized the car behind her. It was Jack's car. When she looked more closely, she noticed Finn, Jack, Tom, and Danny laughing at some unknown joke.

She saw Finn roll down the car window, so she did too. "Hi, did you know that Tom made up that someone ate a carrot and then turned green?" shouted Finn.

"Green! Don't you mean orange?" Amber answered.

"No, that's why it's funny," Finn answered, laughing as he rolled up his window. Amber shook her head, then rolled up her window too. *How was that even funny?* she wondered.

As the van continued on to the airport, Raya dug into her backpack and pulled out a piece of paper. "Look at this picture I painted on Sunday," she said as she held up an exact likeness of her husky, Levi. "Do you like it?" Raya asked.

"Of course! It's amazing," Amber answered. Raya was the best painter in the class. Sometimes she took her paintings to art shows and won awards.

"What should we do the rest of the car ride?" Joy asked shyly.

"Well, we only have fifteen minutes left until we get to the airport," John told them.

"Okay, then how about we sing a song," Joy suggested, forgetting to be shy. Joy loved singing and started them off.

Wonderful things are destined to come,
Falling rain, and torches are glowing brightly,
In the darkening night,
With moonlight to guide them,
On their way across the sky.

Through the zenith and celestial equator,
They make their way down to the horizon.

When the dark sky lights up the colorful house,
Then we shout, yay, the northern lights are here,
And the sky fumes with light and color,
And the stars seem to dance in the sky,
Happily in a merry chorus,
Following their paths across the sky,
To a wonderful world called heaven,
Where angels sing and bagpipes play,
Where happiness rules, and badness drools,
Where spirits sing and bells ring,
And parties stay all day and night,
And cloud beds wait for little sleep,
And golden lights never turn gray,
Where gold is plenty for every spirit to share,
And no one fights or is forced to do things,
Where light is bright in rainbow colors,
And mystical animals leap and play.

By the time the song was finished, everyone in their excitement had joined in, even John.

When they arrived at the airport, all of the kids shouted at the same time, "We're here!" As soon as John stopped the car, the doors flung open and the kids jumped out onto the pavement. Once they had all retrieved their bags from the back of the minivan, John led them into the airport and directed them towards the Delta Airlines check-in line. Once there, they found Ms. Clay, Bob, Julian, and August sitting and waiting for them. "Have you seen the other boys?" asked August, whose dark brown hair, light brown skin, and merry blue eyes made him stand out from the rest of the kids.

"Hmm—no," Raya answered. "Sorry."

"Oh, okay. I'm sure they'll be here soon," August said, then walked away. It wasn't long before the last two groups arrived. Once Ms. Clay had finished her count, confirming all sixteen kids and their chaperones had arrived, she handed out the plane tickets and the group made its way through security.

Once they reached the gate they huddled in a circle. "You must be as quiet as you can on the plane, and be kind to the people who will sell you food. Pick out whatever you want and don't worry, I will pay for it," Ms. Clay reassured them.

"I can still do fashion on the plane, right?" Bella asked. She was obsessed with fashion.

"I guess, but don't get too carried away," said Ms. Clay, smiling. Amber snickered, then covered her mouth so no one would hear her.

After keeping themselves entertained for about twenty more minutes, a voice came over the intercom. "We are about to begin boarding for Delta Flight 1642 to the Manaus Airport in South America, gateway to the Amazon. All ticketed passengers please prepare for boarding." As she spoke, the door to the jetway swung open.

The kids, their teacher and chaperones waited in line,

then when they reached the front scanned their tickets and made their way to the plane. Theirs was going to be a direct flight, and it was on a huge plane. There were three seats on either side, and four in the middle section. The school group was to fill several rows in the middle section of the plane. Ms. Clay led the pack down the aisle to the section where they were to be seated and when they got there said, "Okay everyone. Here we are. You can take any seat you want in the middle section of rows thirty-seven through forty. The adults will be in the aisle seats across from you." Most of the kids had backpacks with them, but their suitcases had been checked, which made finding their seats and getting settled in fairly easy. Amber sat down next to Raya. Other passengers filled the seats, talking loudly. Kids ran around everywhere, trying to pick a seat.

When the commotion died down and all the passengers had found a seat, a flight attendant came over the intercom and said, "We will be pulling back from the gate shortly. All tray tables and seatbacks need to be up, and seatbelts fastened."

The passengers then watched a short safety video as the plane backed away from the gate and made its way to the runway. Once it was their turn, the captain came on the intercom and said, "We are next in line for takeoff. Sit back and enjoy the ride."

The plane jerked, then started down the runway, going faster and faster until it lifted off the ground and soared high into the sky. Amber looked out the window. Everything was as small as toys. Amber imagined she was playing with them and she laughed as the toy train chugged along the mini tracks. Her gaze was immediately turned back to the window, as a bird flew straight towards it, then at the last second turned away.

The day passed by so slowly it was hard not to get bored,

though she and Raya had played headbands almost twenty times, and they memorized every card there was. They had soon gotten bored of that game, and decided to play concentration instead.

"Concentration! Sixty four, no repeats or hesitations. I'll start, you'll follow. Category is—anything. Shows," Raya said.

"Plans," Amber said.

"Arms," Raya said.

"Stuffed animals," Amber said.

"Paint," Raya said.

"The Amazon," Amber said.

"Painting boards," Raya said.

"Lunch!" Amber exclaimed, as the food cart was pushed in front of them.

Raya forgot to say something. "I won!" Amber yelled triumphantly.

"Would either of you young ladies like some food?" asked the tall lady pushing the cart.

"Yes," Raya answered, smiling at having been called a lady.

"Both of you?" the tall lady asked. Amber nodded her head. The lady handed them each a burrito. Amber unwrapped the wax paper that was around hers, and took a bite. It was not very good, but she ate it anyway. She was starving.

After she had finished eating, Amber looked in her notebook filed with facts about the Amazon. A fact caught her eye. It read: How long would it take a plane to fly to the Amazon? The answer below read: two days. *At least this day is almost over,* Amber thought, looking out the window as the plane flew through the clouds. It began to rain, spreading a misty smell throughout the plane. The passengers started to fall asleep, and the plane grew dark as night. Amber checked the time on her watch. It was 10:00 p.m.

It took her a long time to get to sleep because she was mesmerized by the lightning piercing the sky and the rumbling thunder. But finally around 1:00 a.m., she fell into a deep sleep.

When morning light dawned, the storm had passed and bright sunlight streaked across the plane's floor. Amber and Raya woke up around the same time, shortly before the food-cart came again. This time instead of a burrito, Amber got a scone. She bit into it, and it tasted a little bit stale, but she ate it anyway.

The morning passed by slowly, hour by hour, minute by minute, second by second. It was so boring she even got bored with watching the earth below. Amber finally decided to take pictures with her camera. She took pictures of the sky and of the green mass below. As they flew through a cloud, it looked like they were in a whole new world, covered in mist.

The sun-lit clouds grew brighter and brighter. Finally, at Noon, the tall lady brought the cart again. This time she gave them a salad. It wasn't fresh, though it was the best food the airline had provided so far.

Amber's bottom hurt from sitting so long, and her brain was blank. When would this day ever end?

Eventually, the sun slowly began to sink below the horizon, striking the sky with purple and gold. It wasn't long before she was in a deep sleep.

The next thing she knew, the plane was coming in for a landing, and not exactly the kind of landing you'd want to have. Instead of slowing down once it touched down, the plane sped up. Amber heard screaming, lots of screaming, and scraping metal.

By the time the plane stopped, the front end was hanging over a precipice, and the plane was on fire. It started at the front, then drew closer and closer to where Amber sat next to Raya, panic stricken. Amber punched the window, the glass crumbled, and she and Raya squeezed out. Sparks and ashes flew in her face, making her cough. A ball of fire whizzed past her ear, singeing it. She screamed as pain shot through her ear like a sword.

There was mass chaos as one after another, passengers jumped out of the plane and ran down the runway. Amber and Raya eventually found the other kids in their group. Like her own, soot streaked their faces. Amber did a quick count and all sixteen kids were there, but the adults were— missing. "Where is the teacher? Where are the chaperones?"she asked, suddenly more scared than ever.

"The rescue crew took Ms. Clay away to the hospital," Tracy answered.

"What about the other adults?" asked Amber.

"They're over there," said Joy, motioning back towards the plane. Suddenly, the kids saw their chaperones emerging from the smoky scene, and running toward them.

"It's okay, don't panic," May's mom said, as she came upon the group of sooty students.

Then suddenly, a bright light appeared in the sky. It seemed to be coming straight for them, becoming brighter and brighter until all they could see was the light. When the light was almost blinding, a head appeared. The strange head in the sky had three eyes stuck on a chubby, ugly, green face. Suddenly, it spoke. "I am Asgar. I am here to destroy the Power Animals once and for all, and no one will be safe!"

As Asgar spoke, he showed long, pearly-white teeth that gave Amber the shivers. Her blood ran cold as his voice still echoed in her ears. Then she saw and heard Asgar scream, a tiger roar, and then water splashed down on the ground. Afterward, she heard Asgar say, "Ha! I got you!" The light dimmed, and she could see her surroundings once more.

"Did anyone else see Asgar?" Amber asked, shivering again.

Raya came over to stand next to Amber and announced, "Raise your hand if you saw Asgar!"

Amber raised her hand and to her amazement, everyone else in her class did too, including Raya.

"Wait a second! Is it me or were the chaperones just right over there," observed Tom, pointing towards the spot where the adults had been, "and now they are gone?"

This realization was a huge shock to Amber. She and her class were in South America with no grown ups whatsoever!

"What should we do?" she asked.

"We go find the Amazon," Finn answered, pointing towards the greenery in the distance. "That is after all what we came here to do."

"Wait! Let me send a quick message to my mom first," said Amber. She pulled her phone out of her pocket and started typing.

> *Mom,*
> *Our plane has crashed at the edge of the Amazon, but don't worry. I'm okay.*

Before she could type anything else, Raya grabbed her arm and shouted, "Come on, or you're going to get left behind." Amber pushed the send icon on the phone's screen, then followed Raya.

Chapter 3

The Cave

The Amazon jungle is a magnificent broad-leafed rainforest in the heart of Brazil. It covers 1.7 billion acres of land and is home to some of the most numerous and diverse species in the world.

As Amber and her classmates entered the jungle, the description in her notebook came to life. They were only a few feet into the forest and already giant ferns towered over their heads, and there were several monkeys swinging from vines overhead. A wet smell hung in the air, and Amber heard the trickle of water. Blue and yellow macaws flew over their heads in a wide arc, their golden stomach feathers glistening in the sun. As fast as they had come they were suddenly gone.

A big rock that was seven feet tall loomed over their heads. Several large ferns grew upon it. Tiny green plants with four leaves that reminded Amber of clover carpeted the bare ground. Many strong vines entangled, entwined, and encircled the trees. A thick mist covered the greenery. A green and brown-colored milk frog hopped onto a nearby leaf.

"Did you know that the milk frog, when it is scared, produces a white milky liquid from its skin?" Amber asked.

"That's cool," Finn commented.

"Also, the king kinkajou has a prehensile tail, and is related to the raccoon," Amber told them.

"What's a prehensile tail?" asked Joy.

"It's a tail that has adapted to be able to grasp or hold objects," said Amber.

"King kinkajous are so cute," May said.

"Are there any endangered species in the Amazon rainforest?" Joy asked curiously.

"Oh yes!" Amber told her, then said, "Lots! The South African manatee, the uakari monkey, and the giant anteater are all vulnerable. The golden lion tamarin, the pacarana, and the giant otter are endangered; and the rancho grande harlequin frog, glaucous macaw, and the cherry-throated tanager are critically endangered."

"How do you know so much about the Amazon?" asked May.

"This place has been my passion since I was a little kid," said Amber, who instinctively took out her camera, and took picture after picture after picture. Amber remembered that the jungle was delightful, but it also had many dangers. When she looked up at a giant fern, its leaves shook, then a rattlesnake fell from the fern's foliage in front of the class. Hissing, it circled them. August picked up a stick and hit the rattlesnake hard. He then flung the snake into the air and when it landed on the ground several feet away, it hissed and slithered into the rainforest.

"That was a close one," mumbled Amber under her breath.

As the sun began to sink below the horizon, Tracy said, "We need to set up our tent."

"Sorry, that got burned," Bob answered, as if he were happy about that.

"But where will we sleep?" June asked.

"We could sleep in the trees," May suggested.

"But what about the snakes?" Joy asked. "We won't be safe from them."

"I know where we could sleep," Amber announced.

"Where?" the whole class asked at once.

"In a cave," Amber answered.

"But bears will get us in there," Raya complained.

"The only kind of bear the spends time in caves in the Amazon is the spectacled bear," Amber insisted. "It won't bother us."

When the class agreed, they stumbled through the jungle until they finally found a cave. When they entered, they saw a small, spectacled bear asleep on the dirt ground.

The kids each found a spot to rest on the cave floor. Amber lay next to the spectacled bear, the warmth of its fur let her fall into a deep, but troubled sleep.

Chapter 4

Animal Power

When Amber woke up, the birds were chirping and the morning sunlight that filtered through the trees streaked into the cave. Raya got up and whispered, "While we are waiting for the others to wake up, can we sing my new favorite song?"

"I guess so," Amber agreed, and they started to sing.

Wonderful things are destined to come,
Falling rain, and torches are glowing brightly,
In the darkening night,
With moonlight to guide them,
On their way across the sky.

Through the zenith and celestial equator,
They make their way down to the horizon.

When the dark sky lights up with colorful hues,
Then we shout, yay, the northern lights are here,
And the sky fumes with light and color, and the stars,
Seem to dance in the sky,
Happily in a merry chorus,
Following their paths across the sky,

To a wonderful world called heaven,
Where angels sing and bagpipes play,
Where happiness rules and badness drools,
Where spirits sing and bells ring,
And parties stay all day and night,
And cloud beds wait for little sleep,
And golden light never turns gray,
Where gold is plenty for every spirit to share,
And no one fights or is forced to do things,
Where light is bright in rainbow colors,
Where mystical animals leap and play.

Just as they finished their song, a bird let out an alarm call. They walked to the cave's opening and looked out into the Amazon. They saw a salamander sunning itself on a rock, its green and black stripes shifting every so often in the sunlight. A little snake slithered into the sunlight. It hissed contentedly, then curled its body, tucked its head in and fell asleep.

A parrot flew down and pecked seeds off the ground. Amber took a picture of the parrot, the snake, and the salamander. She also had Raya take a picture of her and the spectacled bear. They were having such a good time, they didn't notice their class waking up.

"What should we do?" Joy asked.

"Write a report on fashion to give to Ms. Clay in the hospital?" Bella suggested. Everyone groaned.

"Bella, how are we supposed to get the report to her anyway?" Bob asked.

"Ummm—" Bella hung her head.

"No, we can write a report on the Amazon," Amber said.

"What? You agree to write a report on the Amazon, but not on fashion?" Bella asked outraged.

"Yup! The Amazon is way more fun to write about. And

anyway, maybe if I do this report Ms. Clay will forget about the homework I didn't turn in two days ago," Finn replied.

When everyone agreed, Amber got out her extra notebook and started writing. At the top of the page she wrote, THE ANIMALS OF THE AMAZON RAINFOREST. Under that she wrote: spectacled bear, salamander, snake, parrot, monkey. Then she added some facts and observations.

> *The Amazon rainforest contains huge ferns that block most of the sunlight from making it to the jungle floor. Snakes live in their foliage, and parrots only stop flying to eat. Alligators live in the Amazon, and spectacled bears lumber about. Monkeys swing from vines, and sloths climb the giant ferns. The Amazon River is 4,354 miles long.*

Before she knew it, Amber had filled three pages of her notebook with her report. When she finished writing, she tried to turn on her cellphone, but it didn't work. *Maybe it needs to be charged,* Amber thought, but then she realized there probably wasn't a cellphone tower nearby.

"Did she answer yet?" Raya asked her hopefully as she set down her notebook and pencil.

"I can't even get a signal," Amber told her desperately. "I don't think there is a cellphone tower close enough to make it work."

The way Raya looked at Amber now, she knew that Raya realized she was upset, and was going to try to make her feel better. In truth, right now Amber felt as if she were about to cry.

"Don't worry, we'll find a way to get a message to your mother; and we will find out where all the chaperones went; and we'll get home," Raya told her reassuringly.

Amber desperately hoped she was right, but could not

bring herself to believe it. How could she get a message to her mother? Amber then had an idea. She opened her notebook as fast as she could to a blank page and wrote:

Mom,

Our plane crash-landed and all the chaperones have mysteriously disappeared. We are fighting for survival, and are now stranded in the Amazon rainforest. Help!
Love,
Amber

Then as if by magic, a bird flew over and landed on the rock next to Amber.

"Please take this to my mother," Amber said. "She lives in Baroda, Michigan at 525 Cloud Street."

To her surprise, the bird nodded and took the letter in its beak, unfolded its wings, and flew high, high above them. It flew higher and higher until it was out of sight.

Amber hoped with all her heart that the letter would make it home to her mother. Then Finn's voice broke into her thoughts.

"I'll get a fire going," Finn said.

"No!" Amber shouted.

"Why not?" Tracy asked puzzled.

"It's not like I'm going to set the whole jungle on fire!" Finn laughed.

"I know, but if that does happen, you will kill all the remaining giant ferns!" Amber said.

"Who put you in charge?" Bob asked rudely.

"No one, but she should be," May answered.

"And why is that?" asked Jack.

"Because she knows more about the Amazon than anyone else here," said Sophie.

"Fine, Amber can be in charge," the boys sighed.

"Okay then. August and Finn, go east and look for the Amazon River. Jack, Tom, and Danny, go with Bob, Julian, May, June, and Joy, and go north. Bella, Tracy, Raya, Sophie, and Georgia, go south, and I'll go west," Amber said.

As she left the clearing in the rainforest and headed west, Amber saw a spider monkey swing down on a vine. When it landed next to her, she got out her cellphone and took a picture of it. The monkey then climbed up onto her head and she laughed, then started walking. She didn't even realize that her phone was now getting reception when she texted the picture to her mom along with the message, "My new spider monkey friend."

The spider monkey eventually climbed down her hair, and sat on her shoulder. Amber kept walking until she heard a trickle of water. She followed the sound until she came to a wide river. "Yes, this is it! The Amazon River!" She was about to snap another photo when a message from her mother popped up on her phone. It said, "I just bought my plane tickets. Be there soon."

Just then, a crocodile lifted its head out of the water and snapped its jaws. When it crawled up on the bank, it cornered her by a giant fern. Amber's heart started pounding. *Oh no! It's hungry,* she thought.

The crocodile snapped at her feet. When it bit into the edge of her shoe, Amber felt a sharp pain and pulled her foot away. The crocodile snapped again. Just as its jaws were about to clamp down, the monkey that had been on her shoulder earlier swung down from a vine, grabbed her hand, then swung her away. The crocodile snapped angrily at the air, but caught nothing.

Amber smiled up at the spider monkey and it let out an, "Ooo-ooo Aah-ah" of excitement and swung her into a giant fern. As she looked down at the river below, something caught Amber's eye. It was a baby tiger drowning in the river! She was about to jump in to try and save it, but the spider monkey held her back. It grabbed the vine with one hand, then grabbed her hand, and swung on the vine over the river. With her free hand, Amber grabbed the baby tiger by the scruff of its neck, and once clear of the water the monkey dropped them to the ground.

The mother tiger prowled up. She was huge! "Thank you for saving my daughter," she said. "In return, I will give you the power to talk to animals."

"Is this really happening?" Amber asked. But the mother tiger didn't answer. Instead, her eyes turned green, then a beam of light shot from her eyes, and magic power surrounded the stuffed animal tiger that had been clipped to Amber's backpack. In that moment, the pink heart on the side of Amber's toy began to glow and beat. The beating got louder and louder, and her stuffed animal tiger grew bigger and bigger, then it turned into a real tiger.

"How did you do that?" Amber was dazzled by the mother tiger's power.

"All animals have their own little magic," the mother tiger answered wisely.

"Mm—can I have my stuffed animal back now?" Amber asked.

Light green rays shot from the mother tiger's eyes again, and the tiger shrunk until it was a stuffed animal again.

"Just ask the stuffed animal to turn into a real tiger and it will. Ask it to turn back into a stuffed animal and it will," the wise mother tiger said, then purred softly.

"Okay," Amber said, and hugged her stuffed animal tightly, then started heading back towards the clearing from which she had come. When she met back up with her classmates Finn asked, "So, did anyone find the Amazon?"

"I did!" Amber reported excitedly, then went on to tell

her classmates what had happened. When it finally grew dark and the crocodiles began to wander, Amber and her classmates called it a day, then went back to the spectacled bear's cave to sleep.

When Amber woke up the next morning, there was a letter from her mother sitting next to her on the bed. It had an imprint of a beak on it. Amber laughed as she saw the macaw taking flight outside the cave. Then, she unfolded the letter. It said:

I'm here. Meet me at the airport.
Love, Mom

Amber was overjoyed!

Amber shook Raya awake, and Raya shook Joy awake, and Joy shook May awake, and May shook June awake, and June shook Bella awake, and Bella shook Tracy awake, and Tracy shook Sophie awake, and Sophie shook Georgia awake, and Georgia shook August awake, August shook Julian awake, Julian shook Bob awake, Bob shook Danny awake, Danny shook Tom awake, Tom shook Jack awake, and Jack shook Finn awake.

"Hey, I was having the best dream," Finn said annoyed.

"My mom said she's at the airport now, and she has come to bring us home," Amber said, hope rising in her heart.

"Hey, that's what happened in my dream!" Finn said excitedly.

"Come on, let's go. Amber's mom is waiting," Raya said.

As Amber looked back at the jungle, the mother tiger and her daughter appeared. "Bye," Amber whispered, then took a selfie of herself with the tigers. The kids then hurried back to the airport, and soon left the Amazon behind.

THE END

Tips Kids Can Follow to Help Animals

Several of these tips are from the website:
Petakids.com.

1.   Take everything away with you after you have fun at the beach.

2.   Use a reusable canvas bag, not a plastic one.

3.   Never buy things made from endangered or wild animals.

4.   Only eat fish from a sustainable source.

5.   Reduce, reuse, and recycle!

6.   Support shelters that don't kill animals when they aren't adopted in a certain amount of time.

7.   Feed your pets healthy food.

8.   Never support places or people that hunt for fun.

9.   Be kind to all wildlife, including pets.

10. If an animal is afraid of you, go slow and let it see you be kind to its friends.

11. Help endangered species.

12. NEVER shoot a bird because you want its feathers.

13. NEVER kill an animal even if it hurt you.

14. Support places that treat their animals kindly.

15. If you follow these rules and be kind to animals they won't feel threatened by you, or hurt you.

16. Educate your friends and family about how to help animals.

17. Ask your friends to make birthday donations in your name to the local animal shelter as your gift.

18. Raise money to donate to animals shelters or animal

reserves.

19. Volunteer at your local animal shelter. (Please note, at most places you need to be at least 16 to volunteer).

20. Adopt animals from shelters or animal rescues.

21. Launch a donation drive.

22. Foster an animal.

23. Be kind to animals of all ages.

24. Host a pet craft night.

25. Don't support entertainment that uses animals.

26. Support animals living in the wild.

27. Pledge to be fur free.

28. Put up signs at fishing places that say, "Don't leave fishing line here."

29. Create a fish-friendly sign at your library.

30. Be nice to insects and bugs.

31. Help fight animal testing.

32. Stand up for animals in captivity.

33. Let birds fly free.

34. Pledge to help pigeons.

What Animal Shelters Need

- Water and food bowls
- Grooming tools
- Toys
- Pet beds
- Leashes and collars

How to Create an Animal Saving Group

Bring together a group of your friends who love animals, and name your group. Some ideas for names include the following: The Animal Rescuers, Animal Savers, Feline Rescuers, or anything else you can think of.

Next, find a way to tell each other if an animal is in danger, like calling or texting. Please note that you and your friends will be saving animals from drowning beetles to elephants with broken legs. If you and your friends are up for the challenge, then go right ahead. On your first mission, don't be scared, you can do this!

If the animal is terribly hurt, ask a parent for help. If it's a bee drowning you can easily help it yourself.

Animals need our help. Will you be the one to save the wild? Help me in any way you can to help save endangered species!

Create a Natural Craft

Flower necklaces, headbands and bracelets are some of the easiest crafts to create. All you need to make them are flowers, a sewing needle, scissors, and silk string.

1) Gather a bunch of flowers from your yard, or buy some at a store.

2) Measure your neck, head or wrist to determine how long a piece of string you need.

3) Thread the needle onto the string and pull it so that it is at least 6 inches longer than the measurement you just took.

4) Secure a flower to the end of the string, leaving at least two inches of string at the end.

5) Add additional flowers onto the string. Add them on by pushing the needle through the strongest part of the flower, the stem.

6) Once you have the desired amount of flowers on the string, check to see how it looks on. Once satisfied, tie the final flower to the string as you did with the first flower, leaving at least 2 inches of string at the end.

7) Tie the two ends of the string together, cut off the excess string, then slip on the necklce, headband or bracelet you made and show it off.

Sigma's Bookshelf (www.SigmasBookshelf.com) is an independent book publishing company that exclusively publishes the work of teenage authors, who are between the ages of 13 and 19. The company was founded in 2016 by Minnesota teenager Justin M. Anderson, whose first book, *Saving Stripes: A Kitty's Story*, was published when he was 14, and has since sold hundreds of copies.

"I know there are a lot of other teenagers out there who are good writers and deserve to have their work published, but don't have access to the kinds of resources I do. I wanted to help them," he said.

Sigma's Bookshelf is a sponsored project of Springboard for the Arts, a nonprofit arts service organization. Contributions on behalf of Sigma's Bookshelf may be made payable to Springboard for the Arts and are tax deductible to the extent permitted by law. Donations can be made online at www.SigmasBookshelf.com/donate.

www.ingramcontent.com/pod-product-compliance
Lightning Source LLC
Chambersburg PA
CBHW051930110726
47902CB00002B/480